W9-CHM-888

Magic and Magical Rings other Things

by John Hamilton

VISIT US AT

WWW.ABDOPUB.COM

Published by ABDO Publishing Company, 4940 Viking Drive, Suite 622, Edina, Minnesota 55435.

Printed in the United States.

Editor: Paul Joseph
Graphic Design: John Hamilton
Cover Design: TDI
Cover Illustration: *Cleric* ©1996 Don Maitz
Interior Photos and Illustrations: p 1 *Cleric* ©1996 Don Maitz; p 4 Indian woman wearing rings, Corbis; p 5 *Firelord*, ©1988 Janny Wurts; p 6 *Lord of the Rings* cover, courtesy Houghton Mifflin; p 7 *Demon of the Ring*, ©1980 Don Maitz; p 8 Holy Grail, Corbis; p 9 *Mystic Rose* ©2001 Don Maitz; p 10 (top) Galahad at Grail castle, Corbis; p 10 (bottom) *Sir Percival and the Holy Grail*, Corbis; p 11 Percival on horseback during Grail quest, Corbis; p 12 Abbey's *Galahad Battling the Seven Knights of Darkness*, Corbis; p 13 (top) *Monty Python and the Holy Grail* cover, courtesy Columbia Pictures; p 13 (bottom) Abbey's *Galahad and the Holy Grail*, Corbis; p 14 fortuneteller with crystal ball, Corbis; p 15 *Detect Life Force* ©1996 Don Maitz; p 16 monkey's paw, Corbis; p 17 *Sorcerer* ©1996 Don Maitz; p 18 (top) diary of Tom Riddle, courtesy Warner Brothers; p 18 (bottom) J.K. Rowling, Corbis; p 19 *Force Barrier* ©1996 Don Maitz; p 20 *Jason and the Argonauts*, Corbis; p 21 Francekevich's *Magic Fingers*, Corbis; p 22 Harry Potter with wand, courtesy Warner Brothers; p 23 magic wand, Getty Images; p 24 Stonehenge ceremony, Corbis; p 25 Stonehenge rocks, Corbis; p 26 magic lamp, Corbis; p 27 *Wizard in a Bottle* ©1986 Don Maitz; p 29 witch mixing potion, Corbis.

Library of Congress Cataloging-in-Publication Data

Hamilton, John, 1959–
Magic rings and other magical things / John Hamilton
p. cm. — (Fantasy & folklore)
Includes index.
ISBN 1-59679-337-6
1. Magic—Juvenile literature. 2. Folklore—Juvenile literature. 3. Mythology—Juvenile literature. I. Title

GN475.H26 2005
398.2—dc22

2005048315

Contents

Magic Rings

Rings can hold almost any kind of magical spell in fantasy stories. They can give the bearer the power to heal, invisibility, the ability to stop time, or even bring about the end of the world.

The circle has always been a sacred shape. Shamans and wizards of ancient cultures cast magic circles on the ground or in the air. They believed the circle contained the energy of the person doing the casting. Evil was unable to break this sacred barrier. Also, they believed the circle existed between two dimensions, the real world and the world of magical creatures and gods.

Rings, because they're circles, were believed to have magical powers, especially when blessed by wizards, witches, or shamans. Even today, the names from different countries for the ring finger (the fourth digit on the hand, next to the pinky finger), reflects the ancient belief in the power of the circle, either to heal or create other kinds of magic.

Facing page: Firelord, by Janny Wurts. *Right:* An Indian woman wears gold rings on her fingers.

In European languages such as English, German, and Latin, the ring finger is simply called the *ring finger*, because it is associated with magic rings. In Japan, the ring finger is called *kusuri-yubi*, the medicine finger. Some cultures avoid saying the name of a powerful magic user or god, so they indirectly call the ring finger "nameless." In Finnish, the phrase for ring finger is *nimeton sormi*. In Russian, it is *benzymennyi palets*. Both phrases mean "nameless finger."

In many tales of fantasy and folklore, magic rings play an important part of the story. Many cultures, including the ancient Celts, English, Norse, Germans, Greeks, Romans, Jews, and many Asian cultures, tell stories of heroes who use magical rings on fabulous quests.

One of the most famous magic rings in fantasy stories is the One Ring from J.R.R. Tolkien's *The Lord of the Rings*. The One Ring was forged of gold by the Dark Lord Sauron. In the early days of Middle-earth, there were 19 other Rings of Power given to representatives of the various races who lived in that magical land. Sauron secretly put part of his own soul into the One Ring. When he wore it, he could enslave those who wore the other Rings of Power.

This verse by Tolkien sums up the ownership of the Rings of Power:

Facing page: Demon of the Ring, by Don Maitz.
Below: Front cover of Tolkien's *Lord of the Rings*.

"Three Rings for the Elven-kings under the sky
Seven for the Dwarf-lords in their halls of stone,
Nine for Mortal Men doomed to die,
One for the Dark Lord on his dark throne
In the Land of Mordor where the Shadows lie.
One Ring to rule them all, One Ring to find them
One Ring to bring them all and in the darkness bind them
In the Land of Mordor where the Shadows lie."

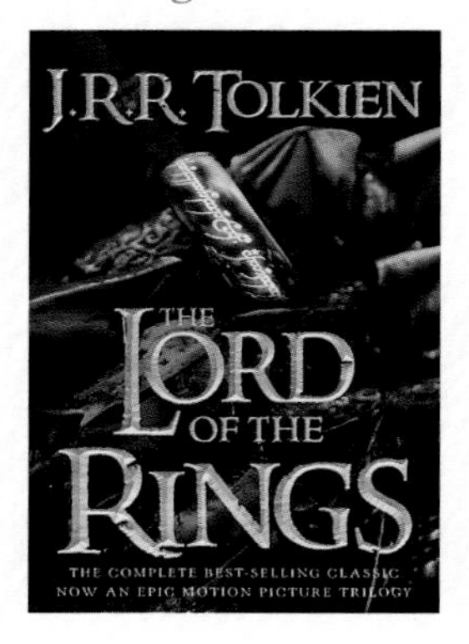

After being lost for centuries, the One Ring fell into the possession of the young hobbit Frodo Baggins. The power of the ring was too great for anyone to use safely. To keep the ring from being recaptured by Sauron, Frodo and eight companions set out from the elf city of Rivendell to the dark lands of Mordor. It is there that Frodo hoped to toss the ring into the volcanic fires of Mount Doom, finally destroying Sauron's evil power.

The Holy Grail

The Holy Grail is part of Christian myths. It was a cup used by Jesus at the Last Supper. It was also used by Joseph of Arimathea to catch Jesus's blood after the Crucifixion. The Grail is said to have special powers. It can heal sicknesses, provide a never-ending supply of food and drink, and even raise the dead.

Myths of a miraculous Grail can be traced back even before Christianity. Legends of the Celts, the ancient people who populated parts of northern Europe, tell of a magical cup, or cauldron, that made the land fertile and restored life to warriors slain in battle.

Over the course of many centuries, the Grail legend has become a blend of many legends, myths, and tales of folklore. The earliest stories don't agree on what the Grail looked like. In some tales, it was a cup. In others, it was a dish, or cauldron, or platter, or even a flat stone.

Left: Some say this is the real Holy Grail, once guarded by the Knights Templar. Other people say it is a hoax.
Facing page: Mystic Rose, by Don Maitz.

Above: Sir Galahad finds himself at the castle of the Holy Grail in this painting by Edwin Austin Abbey.

Over time, the Grail legends found their way into the tales of King Arthur and his British Knights of the Round Table. The very earliest stories tell of a failed quest, or search, for the Grail. In the Welsh poem, *The Treasures of Britain*, a Dark-Ages King Arthur and his knights sail to a far-away land called Annwn. They discover a mysterious crystal castle that revolves on an isle in the middle of a large blue lake. In the center of the castle is a pearl-rimmed cauldron that is said to give eternal life. Arthur and his knights try to carry off the magical cauldron, but the task is too difficult, many knights are killed, and the quest fails. Of the original group, only seven knights, including Arthur, return safely to Britain.

By the 12th and 13th centuries, the Grail legends started to became more consistent. Tales by medieval authors such as Chrétien de Troyes and Robert de Boron blended ancient Celt myths with Christian symbols to create popular French and English stories. By the time Sir Thomas Malory's *Le Morte d'Arthur* was published in 1485, the Grail quest legend had become well established.

Left: Sir Percival and the Holy Grail.
Facing page: Sir Percival on the quest to find the Holy Grail, in a painting by Ferdinand Leeke.

Galahad Battling the Seven Knights of Darkness, by Edwin Austin Abbey.

The Grail story that is most familiar today tells of King Arthur's knights venturing into the wilderness on a sacred quest to find the Holy Grail. A small handful of knights, including Bors and Percival, come close to finding the Grail, but because of their ignorance or their sins on Earth they are not allowed to see it, except in visions. Only Sir Galahad, the best knight and the most pure of heart, is allowed into the inner part of the mysterious Grail castle to gaze on the holy relic. With his quest at an end, life finally leaves Galahad's body, and his soul rises to Heaven.

The legend of the Holy Grail is an ancient one. Its long, complex history has changed through the ages. Even today, countless writers and filmmakers change and add to the story to fit with our modern culture. From stories such as *Excalibur* to *Indiana Jones and the Last Crusade*, from *Monty Python and the Holy Grail* to *The Da Vinci Code*, our fascination with the Holy Grail never seems to end, much like the quest for the Grail itself.

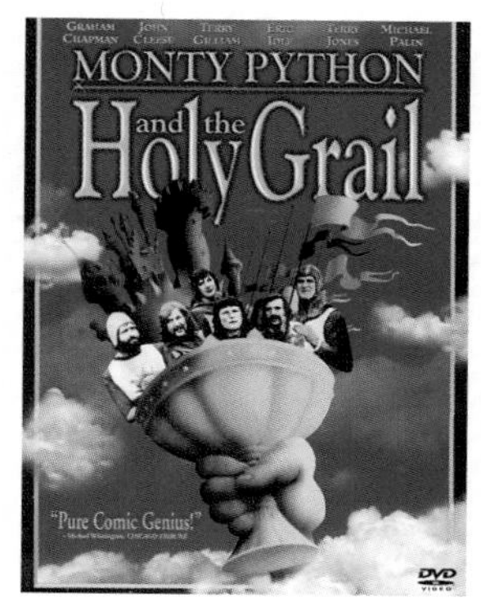

Above: Monty Python gave the Grail legend a humorous twist. Below: *Galahad and the Holy Grail*, by Edwin Austin Abbey.

Crystal Balls

crystal ball is a crystal or glass sphere used by a magician to aid clairvoyance. Clairvoyance is a kind of extrasensory perception, also called ESP. By using a charmed crystal ball, magicians can see things normal people cannot. Gazing intensely into the ball, the witch or wizard can find distant objects or persons, see into the future, or detect magical energies.

Facing page: Detect Life Force, by Don Maitz.
Below: A mysterious fortuneteller seeks an answer in her crystal ball.

In some folktales, a crystal ball is also called a Shew stone. Scrying is the kind of trance that magicians put themselves into in order to see things in the crystal ball. Usually a dark room is needed, with a dim light illuminating the crystal. The ball is a focus for the magician's attention, which removes unwanted thoughts from his or her mind.

Once the right atmosphere is achieved, the magician begins chanting, or saying out loud any words that come into his mind. This is called free-associating. The magician's trance gets deeper and deeper, until he begins to see images and stories, like a movie in his mind. With luck, the answers to the questions he sought are revealed in the trance visions. Sometimes the images even appear on the crystal ball itself, so that others can share in the magician's visions.

Dark Magic

Some sinister objects are filled with magic that seeks to do harm, either to the person possessing the object or to others. For example, in William W. Jacobs's *The Monkey's Paw*, three wishes are granted to whoever possesses a mysterious mummified monkey's paw. Unfortunately, the wishes always have unexpected, and horrifying, consequences. In the story, the evil object is given to a father, mother, and their son. They wish to become rich. The next day, the mother and father are told that their son has been killed in a terrible work accident, and that they will receive money from the company. Next, the mother wishes for her son to come home alive. The father realizes that the monkey's paw will simply bring their son back from the grave, still horribly mangled, a walking zombie. There is a loud knocking at their door. The father hurriedly uses the last wish, and when they open the door, no one is there.

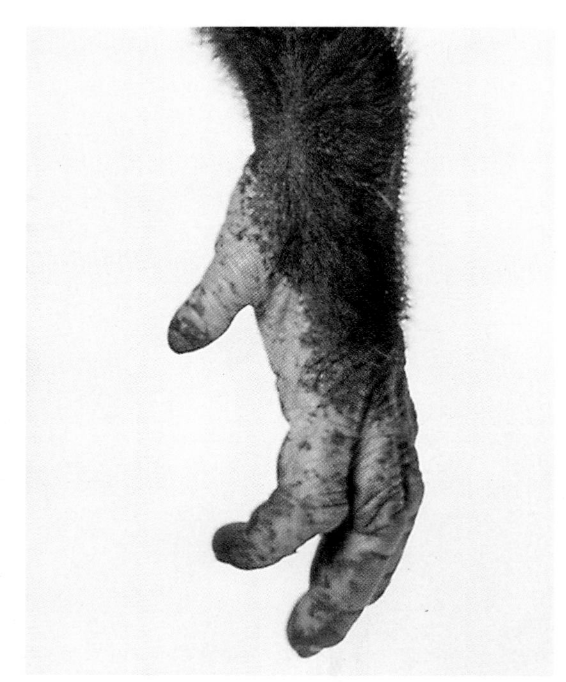

Left: A monkey's paw.
Facing page: Sorcerer, by Don Maitz.

©Maitz
95

In *Harry Potter and the Chamber of Secrets*, the diary of Tom Riddle contains the spirit of the boy who would later become the evil Lord Voldemort. The diary was a horcrux, a magical device created by the worst kind of wizard, one seeking immortality.

A part of a wizard's soul goes into such a device. In this case, part of Tom Riddle's soul went into the magical diary. The diary wrote back to anyone who entered text in its pages, influencing them to do evil deeds.

Above: The diary of Tom Riddle, from *Harry Potter and the Chamber of Secrets. Lower right:* J.K. Rowling, author of the *Harry Potter* series of books. *Facing page: Force Barrier,* by Don Maitz.

In an interview, author J.K. Rowling said of the Riddle diary, "My sister used to commit her innermost thoughts to her diary. Her great fear was that someone would read it. That's how the idea came to me of a diary that is itself against you. You would be confiding everything to pages that aren't inanimate."

The idea of an evil witch or wizard keeping parts of their soul in a dark magic object isn't a new one. The concept is told in many folktales all over the world. In Russian myths, the evil spirit Koschei the Deathless kept his soul in a needle. "His soul is hidden separate from his body inside a needle, which is in an egg, which is in a duck, which is in a hare, which is in an iron chest, which is buried under a green oak tree, which is on the island of Bujan, in the ocean." As long as the needle containing his soul is safe, Koschei cannot die.

© MAITZ 95

Right: A scene from *Jason and the Argonauts*, with Jason fighting the "children of the hydra's teeth." *Facing page: Magic Fingers*, by Al Francekevich.

Dead body parts are often used to hide dark magic. Shrunken heads and crystal skulls are frequently seen in fantasy stories. Even teeth can hold evil spells. In *Jason and the Argonauts*, the villain scattered the teeth of a slain creature, called a hydra, onto the ground. The "children of the hydra's teeth" sprang from the earth. They were skeletons, armed with swords, ready to do the bidding of their evil master.

A folktale of the 19th century tells of the peculiar "hand of glory." Late one stormy evening, a traveler arrived at an inn and begged to stay the night. The owner of the inn agreed, but since all the rooms were full, the traveler would have to stay in the main hall, next to the fireplace. The owner was suspicious of the stranger, and ordered a servant girl to stay up and spy on him.

The servant girl, hidden in the shadows, almost fell asleep. Then she noticed the stranger get up and take an object out of a bag. It was a dry, withered hand, severed from its owner many years ago. The horrified girl watched as the traveler put a thick substance, like wax, on each fingertip of the hand, and then lit the fingers. The man set the hand down on a table and chanted, "Let those who are asleep, stay asleep." Then he started going into the rooms of the inn and stealing the guest's possessions.

The servant girl tried to wake her master, but the magic spell kept him fast asleep, along with everyone else in the inn. Finally, the girl poured a jug of milk on the burning hand, extinguishing the flames. At that moment, everyone woke up and chased the evil burglar away.

WANDS

A wand is a straight, hand-held stick often used by witches and wizards to cast spells. The wand focuses the user's magical energy like a lens. The more powerful the witch or wizard, the more effective is the wand. Wizards often use a larger variation of a wand called a staff. The wizard Gandalf, from J.R.R. Tolkien's *The Hobbit* and *The Lord of the Rings,* often used a staff to perform his powerful magic.

Wands are usually made of wood, but are sometimes made of metal or crystal instead. Some magicians make a wand simply by snapping off a twig from a tree. Others buy special types of wood from a store, and then customize their wands with decorations, often adding mystic runes and symbols to make the wands more potent.

In J.K. Rowling's fantasy world of *Harry Potter*, wizards and witches use custom-made wands depending on the personalities of the wizards, and the kinds of spells they want to cast. No two wands are alike. Wands are bought at Mr. Ollivander's store in Diagon Alley. New students to Hogwarts are measured to find the best wand that fits their personality. Mr. Ollivander says that it is really the wand that chooses the wizard.

As the white-haired shopkeeper once explained to Harry Potter, "Every Ollivander wand has a core of a powerful magical substance, Mr. Potter. We use unicorn hairs, phoenix tail feathers, and the heartstrings of dragons. No two Ollivander wands are the same, just as no two unicorns, dragons, or phoenixes are the same. And of course, you will never get such good results with another wizard's wand."

Harry eventually bought a wand made of holly wood, with a single phoenix feather. Mysteriously, the evil Lord Voldemort also had a wand with a phoenix feather core, a fact that would later haunt Harry in his adventures.

Facing page: A magic wand. *Below:* Harry Potter uses a magic wand that has a single phoenix tail feather at its core.

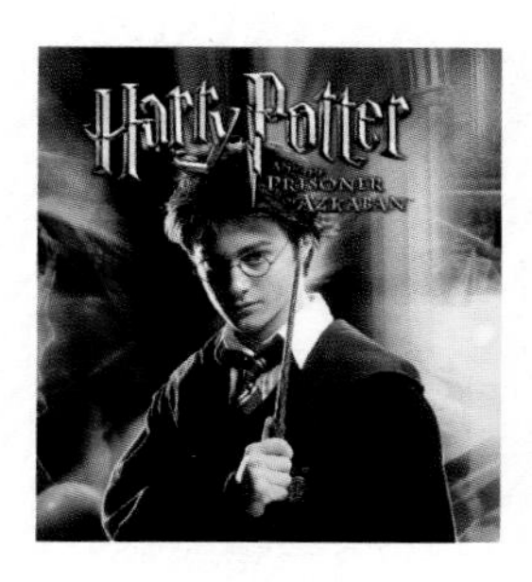

Stonehenge

tonehenge is an ancient monument that stands in the English countryside north of the city of Salisbury, in Wiltshire, southern England. It is a collection of huge standing stones set in a series of concentric circles, surrounded by mounds of earthworks. It is very old. Parts of Stonehenge date back more than 5,000 years.

Stonehenge was almost certainly a place of worship for the people who built it. Some think it was used by Druids or Romans, but historians say neither of those cultures existed in the area at the time the monument was constructed.

The stone pillars used to create the monument weigh up to 50 tons (45 metric tons) each. The stones are arranged in a precise pattern so that the angle of the northeast entrance to the circles exactly matches the midsummer sunrise (the summer solstice). Some of the rocks were probably taken from a quarry in southwestern Wales, more than 240 miles (386 km) away. The massive stones had to be brought to the site by sea, river, or overland. It was an amazing construction project for its time.

Many people think Stonehenge is a magical place. The legends of King Arthur say that the wizard Merlin first discovered the Giants' Ring (Stonehenge) in Ireland, and then had it magically transported to its current location on the Salisbury Plain.

Facing page: The mysterious Stonehenge. *Below:* The site was probably used for religious purposes by ancient cultures.

Lamps and Bottles

Bottles and lamps in folklore are often charmed, or cursed, depending on the circumstances. Some bring good luck to those who are worthy, but calamity to people who are greedy or wicked. More significantly, it isn't the lamps and bottles themselves that are important, but what's *inside*.

Spirits of many varieties can live in bottles and lamps. Often they're trapped by strong magic, a slave to whoever cast the spell ensnaring them. But as many characters find out, to their misfortune, the spirits are clever and often turn the tables on their greedy masters.

Facing page: Wizard in a Bottle, by Don Maitz.
Below: A magic lamp.

By far the most well-known example of a spirit in a lamp is the genii trapped inside the magic oil lamp in the story of Aladdin, from *The Book of One Thousand and One Nights*. Aladdin was employed by a powerful sorcerer to retrieve a plain oil lamp from an enchanted cavern. When the sorcerer tried and failed to double-cross Aladdin, the young man kept the lamp for himself. Aladdin then discovered, to his astonishment, that evil spirits called geniis (or djinns) lived in the bottle. The geniis had to obey whoever owned the lamp.

Aladdin, who came from a poor family, used the geniis to become wealthy, build a fabulous palace, and eventually marry the sultan's beautiful daughter. The jealous sorcerer returned and tried to steal back the lamp, but the clever Aladdin defeated him. Aladdin then went on to live a long, happy life.

Magic Potions

A potion is a magical liquid, a type of medicine or poison created by a witch or wizard. Potions usually must be drunk to take effect, but sometimes a drop on the skin will do. Potions are most often used to heal illnesses. In 19th century America and Europe, wandering charlatans sold potions they claimed would heal almost any kind of sickness.

In tales of fantasy, potions are often used to charm or bewitch unknowing victims. Potions are especially popular for making people fall in love with one another. In addition to love potions, there are also hate potions to break apart lovers.

Potions are usually mixed in big metal pots called cauldrons. Their ingredients can be bizarre and hard-to-find items, such as the eye of a newt, or a witch's laugh. Mixing a potion can be complicated, and takes special training.

In the fantasy world of J.K. Rowling's *Harry Potter* books, students at Hogwarts School of Witchcraft and Wizardry learned how to make potions from Severus Snape. He was the Potions Master for the first several books in the series.

Snape once told a class of wizards-in-training, "I don't expect you will really understand the beauty of the softly simmering cauldron with its shimmering fumes, the delicate power of liquids that creep through human veins, bewitching the mind, ensnaring the senses… I can teach you how to bottle fame, brew glory, even stopper death—if you aren't as big a bunch of dunderheads as I usually have to teach."

Facing page: A witch mixes ingredients in a cauldron for a magic potion.

Glossary

CAULDRON

A large metal pot, with a lid and handle, used to cook food over an open fire. Cauldrons are often a convenient kind of pot in which to mix magic potions. Some historians think the Holy Grail may have been a small cauldron, rather than a cup.

CLAIRVOYANCE

The ability to tell what will happen in the future, or to perceive things beyond the normal senses, like seeing or hearing. People with clairvoyance are said to have a sixth sense, second sight, or extrasensory perception (ESP).

CRUCIFIXION

The killing of Jesus Christ. People were crucified by being nailed or bound to a wooden cross and then left to die.

CRUSADES

A series of military expeditions launched by several European countries in the 11th, 12th, and 13th centuries. The main goal of the Crusades was to recapture territory in the Holy Land from Muslim forces, but there were also many other political and religious reasons for the wars.

FOLKLORE

The unwritten traditions, legends, and customs of a culture. Folklore is usually passed down by word of mouth from generation to generation.

KNIGHTS OF THE ROUND TABLE

The legendary group of knights who swore loyalty to King Arthur and who lived at the castle of Camelot. The Round Table was a large table where many knights could sit together in a circle. In that way, no one knight was more important than another. In addition to King Arthur, some of the most famous knights who sat at the Round Table included Sir Lancelot, Sir Gawain, Sir Gareth, Sir Kay, Sir Bedevere, Sir Bors, Sir Bedevire, and Sir Galahad.

MEDIEVAL
Something from the Middle Ages.

MIDDLE AGES
In European history, a period defined by historians as roughly between 476 A.D. and 1450 A.D.

NORSE
The people, language, or culture of Scandinavia, especially medieval Scandinavia.

QUEST
A long, difficult search for something important. When the knights of Camelot were searching for the Holy Grail, they were said to be on a quest.

RELIC
An object from an earlier time. Relics usually have some kind of historical or sentimental importance. The Holy Grail is an example of a relic.

SHAMAN
A person who performs an ancient form of magic called shamanism. They used a special knowledge of nature to help their tribes. Shamans believed they could heal, communicate with plants and animals, and walk between this world and the mystical world. Shamans often went into deep trances to perform their magic. There is archaeological evidence of shamanism reaching back 40,000 years.

TRANCE
A kind of hypnotic mental state. A person in a trance doesn't seem to be affected by interruptions from the outside world. Instead, he seems to be intensely concentrating on something, sometimes chanting phrases over and over. People in a trance are said to be more open to experiencing clairvoyance.

UNICORN
A mythical beast that looks like a horse with a single, sharp horn that projects out of its forehead.

INDEX